Hattie
and the Fox

by Mem Fox
Illustrated by Patricia Mullins

Simon & Schuster Books for Young Readers

Hattie was a big black hen.
One morning she looked up and said,
"Goodness gracious me!
I can see a nose in the bushes!"

"Good grief!" said the goose.
"Well, well!" said the pig.

"Who cares?" said the sheep.
"So what?" said the horse.
"What next?" said the cow.

And Hattie said,
"Goodness gracious me!
I can see a nose
and two eyes in the bushes!"

"Good grief!" said the goose.
"Well, well!" said the pig.
"Who cares?" said the sheep.
"So what?" said the horse.
"What next?" said the cow.

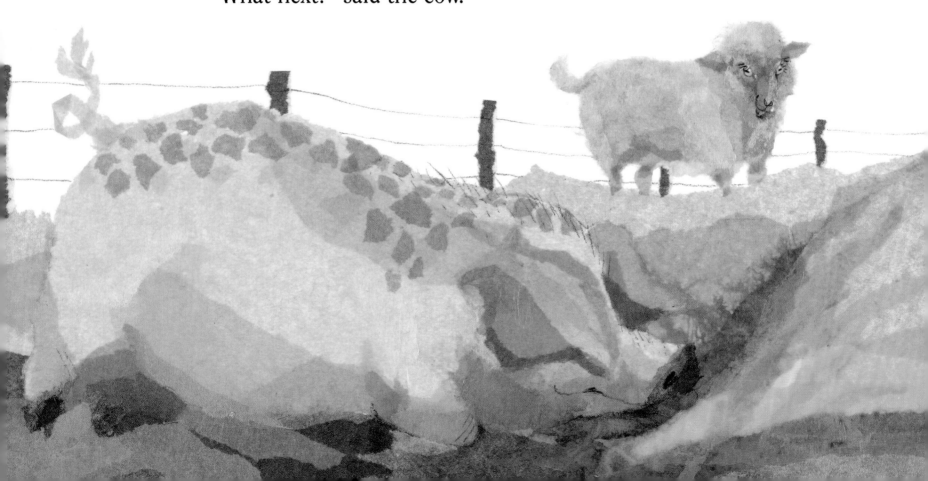

And Hattie said,
"Goodness gracious me!
I can see a nose, two eyes,
and two ears in the bushes!"

"Good grief!" said the goose.
"Well, well!" said the pig.
"Who cares?" said the sheep.
"So what?" said the horse.
"What next?" said the cow.

And Hattie said,
"Goodness gracious me!
I can see a nose, two eyes, two ears,
and two legs in the bushes!"

"Good grief!" said the goose.
"Well, well!" said the pig.
"Who cares?" said the sheep.
"So what?" said the horse.
"What next?" said the cow.

And Hattie said,
"Goodness gracious me!
I can see a nose, two eyes, two ears, two legs,
and a body in the bushes!"

"Good grief!" said the goose.
"Well, well!" said the pig.
"Who cares?" said the sheep.
"So what?" said the horse.
"What next?" said the cow.

And Hattie said,
"Goodness gracious me!
I can see a nose, two eyes, two ears, a body, four legs,
and a tail in the bushes!
It's a fox! It's a fox!"
And she flew very quickly into a nearby tree.

"Oh, no!" said the goose.
"Dear me!" said the pig.
"Oh, dear!" said the sheep.
"Oh, help!" said the horse.

But the cow said, "MOO!"

so loudly that the fox was frightened and ran away.

And they were all so surprised
that none of them said anything
for a very long time.

SIMON & SCHUSTER BOOKS FOR YOUNG READERS
An imprint of Simon & Schuster Children's Publishing Division
1230 Avenue of the Americas
New York, New York 10020

First American Edition 1987
Text copyright © 1986 by Mem Fox
Illustrations copyright © 1986 by Patricia Mullins
All rights reserved including the right of reproduction
in whole or in part in any form.
Simon & Schuster Books for Young Readers is a trademark of
Simon & Schuster.

Printed and bound in China
15

Library of Congress Cataloging-in-Publication Data
Fox, Mem, 1946- Hattie and the fox.
Summary: Hattie, a big black hen, discovers a fox in the bushes, which
creates varying reactions in the other barnyard animals.   [1. Chickens—
Fiction.   2. Foxes—Fiction.   3. Domestic animals—Fiction]   I. Mullins,
Patricia, 1952- ill.   Title   PZ7.F8273Hat   1986   [E]   86-18849
ISBN 0-02-735470-9

Hattie and the Fox was originally published in Australia
in 1986, by Ashton Scholastic.